KAMSI

THE PSYCHIC ONES

THE PSYCHIC ONES

Published by JDD Books
+447309255086

Book Illustrations by
Nana Agyekum Oppong
heneagyekum@gmail.com

Table of Contents

CHAPTER 1

Preparations

Fwoosh! The flame soared faster and more accurately and hit the target perfectly. He threw another in the air and zapped it with a large streak of lightning. It exploded, destroying all the targets in one go. However, that was not enough to get him into TIMS (The International Mage School). To do so, he would not only have to get above 90% in the physical tests but also the writing test. He finished off his battle techniques and took off his ring.

"Garret, dinner is ready. Eat quickly please, the festival starts at 5 !" His mum shouted.

"The Festival!" he thought to himself. During the festival every mage at the age of 14 will get to choose 2 magic types out of the following 8. Fire, Ice, Lightning, Wind, Earth, Water, Light, and Dark. Very few people have the ability to master light and dark so it is an unpopular choice. After choosing your 2 types you are then able to study them in depth, possibly learning how to use other branches of elements such as acid and metal. Once every decade 1 mage chosen at random is given the ability to master all elements at an expert level and is destined to save the world.

It was enormous and beautiful beyond

description. Everyone in the city was gathered around, the lights and music made it so relaxing despite the magnitude of the crowd. Garret gasped... There he was, his idol. The Dark Light (wizard name) was here. TDL (The Dark Light) was the first mage to ever master both light and dark. In addition to that, he was the strongest and most popular. The crowd went crazy at the sight of him. He hushed them down and after giving a few autographs and pictures, he began his speech.

FESTIVAL

CHAPTER 2

The Festival

"Dear mages of Draven city, today is a momentous day as it is the Mastery Festival. As well as that, one of you will be chosen to save the world. This day means ..... you must make sure that you ..... anybody who doesn't can .... SLAP!

"Garret Retvic! Wake up this instant! The speech wasn't that long. You have to pick your magic types now." his mum whispered.

His eyes snapped open and he looked

around him. Everyone else was meditating and he could see the 2 magic sigils above their heads switching and turning. He immediately shut his eyes and began to choose his types. It would be over quickly he already knew what he was going to choose: Fire and Lightning. Right? He thought. But then, Ice would be pretty cool and earth as well, he could even give a shot at light, or maybe dark. As he continued to ponder on his choices, the elements disappeared and he was woken from his meditation...

Wait, WAIT! He hadn't picked his choices **He hadn't picked his choices!** Has this ever happened before? He instantly panicked, the realisation hit him hard. The whole point of choosing the 2 magic types was that you could master them without your rings. The rings would deactivate after the festival as you should have picked your choices, but he didn't. Did that mean he didn't have magic? He tried to summon a small flame and failed. He was about to whisper to his mum when he was interrupted by the loud voice of The Dark Light.

"So I assume that you all have picked your choices." The crowd cheered with excitement. "But just to make sure, is there anyone who hasn't made their choices yet?"

Garret slowly raised his hand, scanning the crowd, hoping that there would be someone else to share his embarrassment with. There was, he couldn't believe it. It was Darvyn Caldor and Narvari Jae-Blynn, his 2 best friends. He gasped with relief, he wasn't alone. He returned his gaze to The Dark Light.

"So, you three boys didn't make your

choices, humph!. Come with me at the end of the festival, there is something I must show you. You are in a great deal of trouble!. He turned to the crowd....."people, let the celebration begin!"

The crowd cheered and the music started. Food was being served and people danced and celebrated. Fireworks went off and the sky was glittered with amazing colours. The smell of pancake with honey syrup and lemon wafted through his nose but he wasn't in the mood to get it. "You are in a great deal of trouble!" he thought to himself. Could it really be that bad? What was he going to do? Would he execute them or maybe exile them after all they didn't have magic. But he wouldn't worry about that now as there was a festival going on and he couldn't afford to miss the fun.

For the following 3 hours he really enjoyed himself. He had a lot of pancakes and played loads of games with his friends and soon had forgotten what TDL had said. He played some water sports in the magic pool and helped to set up some fireworks. By the time the festival was over, he was drenched in sweat and out of breath. Then he remembered what TDL had said.

"Come with me at the end of the festival"

CHAPTER 3

Chosen or not

He called Darvyn and Narvari over. They looked at each other warily.

"I guess we have to go now." Narvari sighed. "We might as well get it done as soon as possible."

"What is there to worry about, I mean he can't be that bad. Could he?" Darvyn chuckled.

"What if we are the chosen ones?" he gasped.

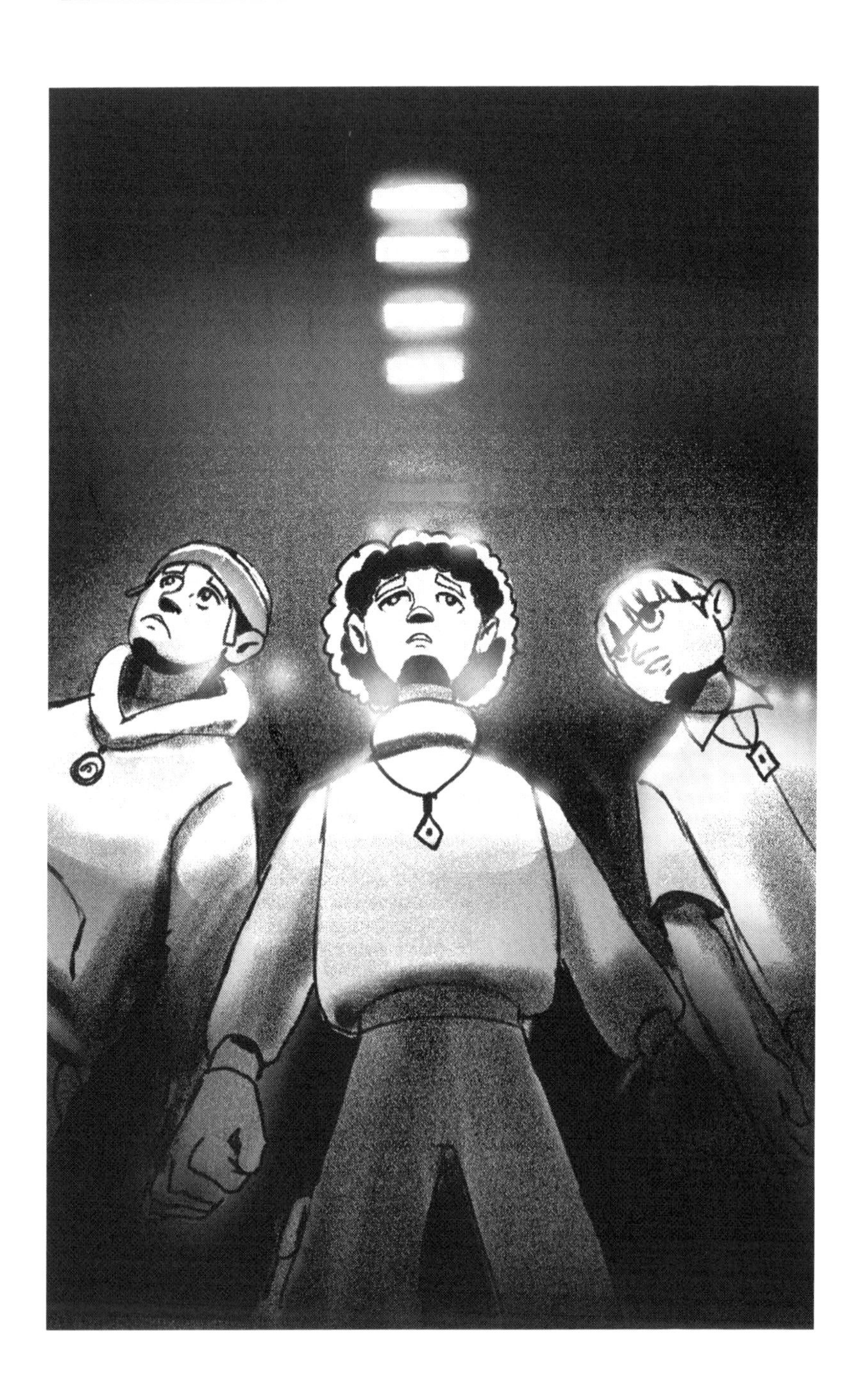

A smile formed on their faces and they rushed towards the building where TDL was waiting.

The Dark Light smiled "Hello boys, there is something I must show you."

Garret eagerly asked "Are we the -

"NO. You are not the chosen ones. As you asked, I might as well tell you the truth."

They looked at each other in confusion. The truth? They had been lied to!

"So, for the past few decades, the chosen ones have been taken hostage by Aeron-

"AERON!! Isn't he that evil grand mage that you defeated, isn't he supposed to be dead!" Darvyn shouted.

"Yes and no. I did defeat him but just before he died, he gave his powers onto his son Aeron junior (Jnr). He was already a powerful mage so with the powers he was given, he was able to defeat and capture some of the chosen ones. From some information gathered we have found out that Aeron junior has a weapon that can freeze you and strip you of your ability to use magic. After seeing what this weapon could do, the Council of Mages decided to look into the future one last time to see whether there would be anyone who could stop him. But instead of looking into the future, they ended up finding an old prophecy basically saying that on this day 3 young mages would lose their magic to gain a new type, to defeat Aeron Jnr." The Dark Light said.

They stood there in shock, trying to absorb the information that had just been thrown at them. They were going to get a new magic type; they would have to defeat Aeron Jnr. They didn't even know what he looked like let alone where he was.

"Chop chop, you have to gain your powers now." The Dark Light said. They followed him into a room where three purple contact lenses were kept on three different chairs with their names on it. Garret put on his contact lens and a spine-tingling sensation shot through his body, then his eyes burned as if someone had put a drop of lava in them. The pain lasted for a few seconds before it went away. He looked up to see his friends suffering from the same thing as him.

After they were done TDL said "Now boys you can go and select one of the 3 types of psychic powers you would like, the contact lenses in your eyes are not only permanent but also are trackers so that we can send support if necessary. Now you have two weeks to learn how you use your powers before the Council of Mages calls you back for your mission. Don't worry; your parents have already been informed of your situation. Good Luck."

They looked at each other and left the room. "So, I guess we pick our powers now." Garret said. "Let's see, I can be offence, Narvari you can be support and Darvyn defence, right?"

They all agreed in unison and set off back to their homes.

CHAPTER 4

Never gets easier

ZIP, SLASH, BOOM! Garret summoned a barrage of swords piercing the target and destroying it. Narvari created an invisibility bubble and snuck behind the walls to heal Garret.

"Wow these training robots sure aren't any easy task," he chuckled.

Suddenly they heard a loud voice.

"Training robot ultimate move incoming, please... please prepare appropriately!" it said.

They peeked around the wall to see the robot charging up a final move. Was that a meteor strike, it was coming down fast and they didn't have a lot of time. They rushed over to Darvyn. Using his magic, he set up a protection dome. Narvari realising that it would not hold, powered him up to make it even stronger. Now they would just have to wait.

The strike came down harder than expected. They could feel the heat from within them; however, Darvyn was struggling even more . Garret could see the sweat and strain on his face, his shirt was smouldering and his muscles bulging. He was putting in so much work and all they could do was sit there. Just as they thought it was over, they saw one last meteor falling. Darvyn's shield broke and Garret realised he had to do something. If he could destroy it before it hit, they would be saved. He flew up into the sky and hit it with all he had. He flung through swords and fireballs, shot large streams of lightning, he even tried to blow it off course but none of that worked. He remembered the special move he had been working on; a concentrated blast of psychic energy. It would take a lot of his energy, so he needed to make it count. He cleared his mind and placed his hands together. He conjured as much power as he could and blasted it out trying to keep it as concentrated as possible. It zipped through the air passing through.

He fainted as he floated down but luckily he was caught by Narvari. He healed Garret and Darvyn, and they left the arena.

"Geez, it never gets easier," he sighed. "I

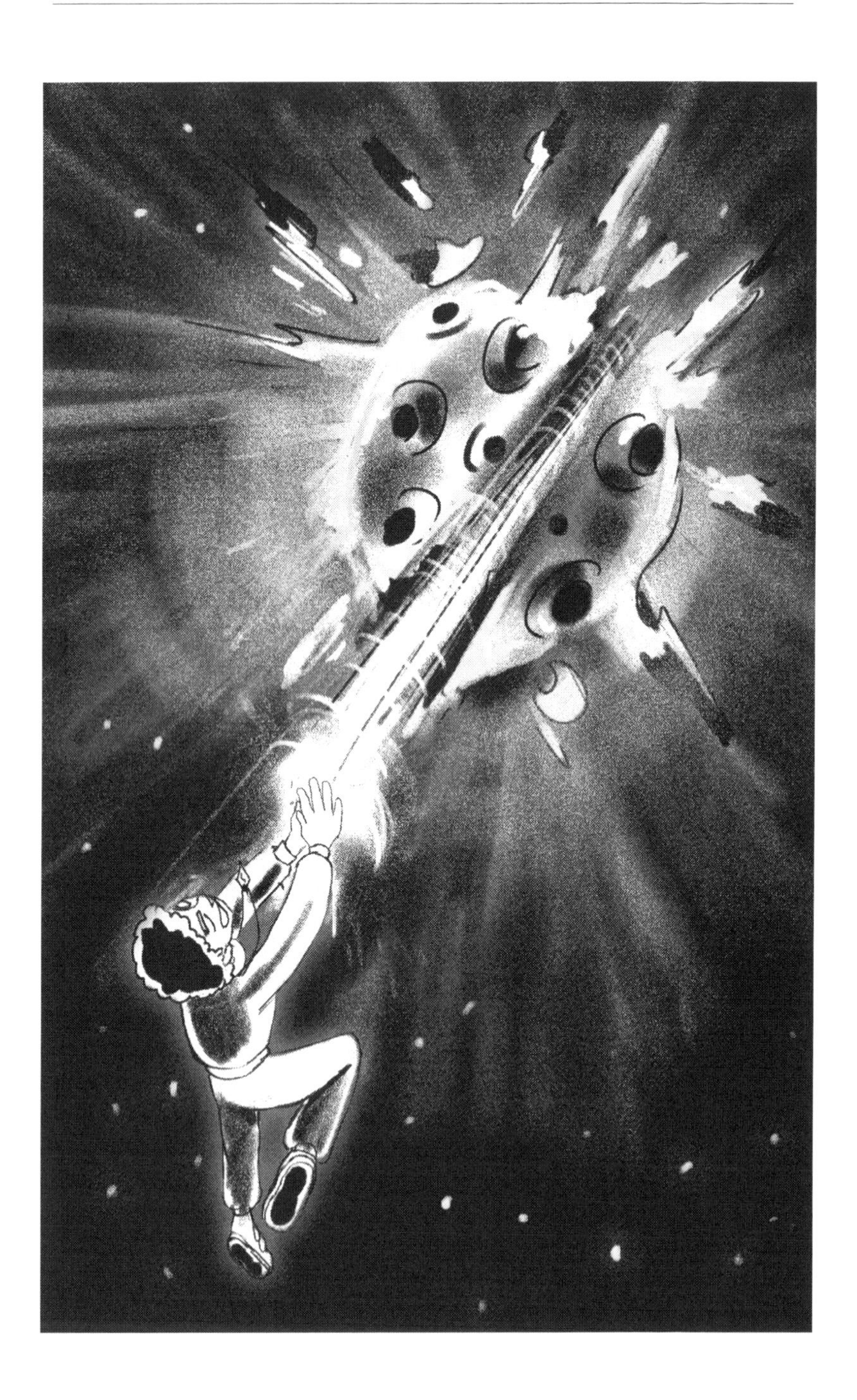

wonder if we will be able to stop Aeron Jnr."

"We sure will! Narvari will just turn us invisible, then Garret, you shoot him with that laser-beam-thing of yours and he will be taken down. We will take him down so fast his generals won't even notice!" Darvyn shouted.

As they walked out of the arena, they saw a strange looking eye in the sky, but they thought nothing of it.

CHAPTER 5

An eye in the sky

"Please, defeat me. ME! Ha! You think that would be possible, I have whole legions at my disposal. I am the greatest mage ever!" Aeron Jnr shouted.

He turned away from his glass eye; he already knew what those boys could do. They weren't worth his time.

"General, prepare a small assassination squad. We will be having visitors soon. Oh and make sure they are psychic resistant." he said.

CHAPTER 6

An early call

RING...RING. RING...RING!

"Garret. Someone is calling you. Oh, it's The Dark Light. Come and answer it!"

"At this time." He sighed. Dragging himself out of bed, he answered the call.

"Hello," he whispered.

"The time is now!" TDL shouted.

"Time for what?" he queried.

"The portal is opened for you to enter Aeron Jnr's lair," TDL announced. "Hurry up, your friends are waiting!"

He jumped out of his room and flew into the kitchen, finishing his breakfast in less than 3 minutes. He zipped into the shower and got ready in 5 minutes. After saying his final goodbyes to his parents, he ran to his rendezvous.

Upon arrival, his friends greeted him and gave him the information on what the lair looked like. After they had discussed the route with each other, TDL walked in. With no explanations necessary he placed down the portal. The 3 boys looked at each other and walked into a new adventure.

CHAPTER 7

The frightful fortress

A gargantuan base loomed over them. Turrets were placed everywhere and there was a massive skull placed on the top of a tower. The sky was dark, and lightning streaked through the clouds. The boys shivered- it was cold, and they had brought no warm clothes. As they looked for a way into the lair, a horde of large spiders attacked them. Garret shot a laser beam destroying three in one go. Then he summoned an electric staff and smashed the rest of them. They hurried into a small passageway in the side of the building to escape any more monsters.

"So according to the map we have, there are three floors. Each floor is more densely guarded with stronger monsters. So, for the first and maybe second we need to avoid combat so that we don't get injured," Narvari whispered.

"Ok then it shouldn't be too hard -

"All monsters be on your highest alert; the psychics have entered the lair"

"Maybe a bit harder then, but we should still be fine." Darvyn chuckled.

They ducked behind a wall just before a guard spotted them. They slipped through the shadows, hiding from view. As they crossed a large pathway a group of guards saw them and started to chase them. They ran as fast as they could and tried to avoid more trouble, but they couldn't. More monsters saw them and soon they were being chased by a horde of enemies.

The general shouted "Close the doors to floor 2! It is an emergency!"

Oh dear! That wasn't good. Now they really had to run. They ran faster, with their stamina disappearing faster than ever. They were getting closer to the exit, but it still seemed miles away. He looked to his right to see Darvyn falling back and Narvari almost out of breath. The enemies were catching up. One of them jumped beside him and threw a punch that would have knocked him over. He dodged it by millimetres and gave the monster a quick shove. It fell over and was trampled by the large horde of other monsters.

He continued to run when an idea popped into his head.

"Darvyn! Narvari! Grab onto me, I have an idea and if it doesn't work then we won't be making it out of here."

They held on tightly as Garret concentrated. He created a replica of a jetpack and blasted them forward. The door was about to close when they whizzed through, barely making it. Barely making it. Garret looked behind him to see his arm about to be crushed by the door. Would he lose his whole arm ? The mission had barely started!

Suddenly it felt as if time slowed. Could it be a secret power he had? or maybe his arm had already been crushed and he had fainted from the pain, or maybe it was a dream. Nevertheless, dream or not, he didn't want to get his arm crushed . He created a small pole in his hand turning it vertically. He widened its structure just as the time returned to normal. He quickly pulled his hand as the wall was held open. But even that wasn't enough to stop it; the wall shut with a deafening BOOM and sealed the three boys off from the rest of the monsters.

CHAPTER 8

Don't give up

The elevator slowly went up, taking the boys to the next floor. They stood in silence realising that this wasn't going to be as easy as they thought. They were nearing the top floor, but no one wanted to speak, so Darvyn did. "Come on boys, cheer up. I know that might have been a close call, but we still have two more floors to go. We are not going to make it out alive like this."

So, they formulated a plan and set out to

reach the third floor.

CHAPTER 9

The Mechs

Garret hurried forward, hands on his silent sniper. After a short while of trial and error he had managed to create a perfect silencer. It would be completely silent when fired. He snapped off his thoughts when he heard a sound, putting his eye to scope, he found their first enemy. It seemed like a guard of some sort; it was working with some controls. Maybe they would be able to find a shortcut with it. He aimed and took fire. WHIZZ! The guard went down, and they moved forward sneaking with efficiency and grace as if they were trained military. They heard footsteps and Narvari quickly created an invisibility bubble. They rushed into the room and quietly shut the door.

"Phew, we're safe here. So now we can find out the way to get to the 3rd floor quickly." Narvari said.

"Keep your voice down!" Garret whispered. "They might hear us!"

"It's fine the bubble not only makes us invisible, but it also stops any sound from getting out. Quite smart, I know." Narvari chuckled smugly.

"Oh guys, I found these mechs that we can activate. I think that we can use it to get to floor 3." Darvyn called.

"Oh nice but let me just prove to Garret

how good my bubble is. GUARDS, GUARDS. IF YOU CAN HEAR ME, WE ARE IN THE CONTROL ROOM FIGURING OUT A WAY TO ESCAPE!" Narvari bellowed. "See they didn't hear a - BANG BANG! Two foot shaped imprints dented the wall. SMASH!. The metal door started to bend.

"NARVARI, you idiot!. What were you thinking, now what are we going to do?"

"Do not fear, my friends, for our mechs are here." Darvyn smiled.

The door was hit again and just at that moment. The mechs flew down from three tubes.

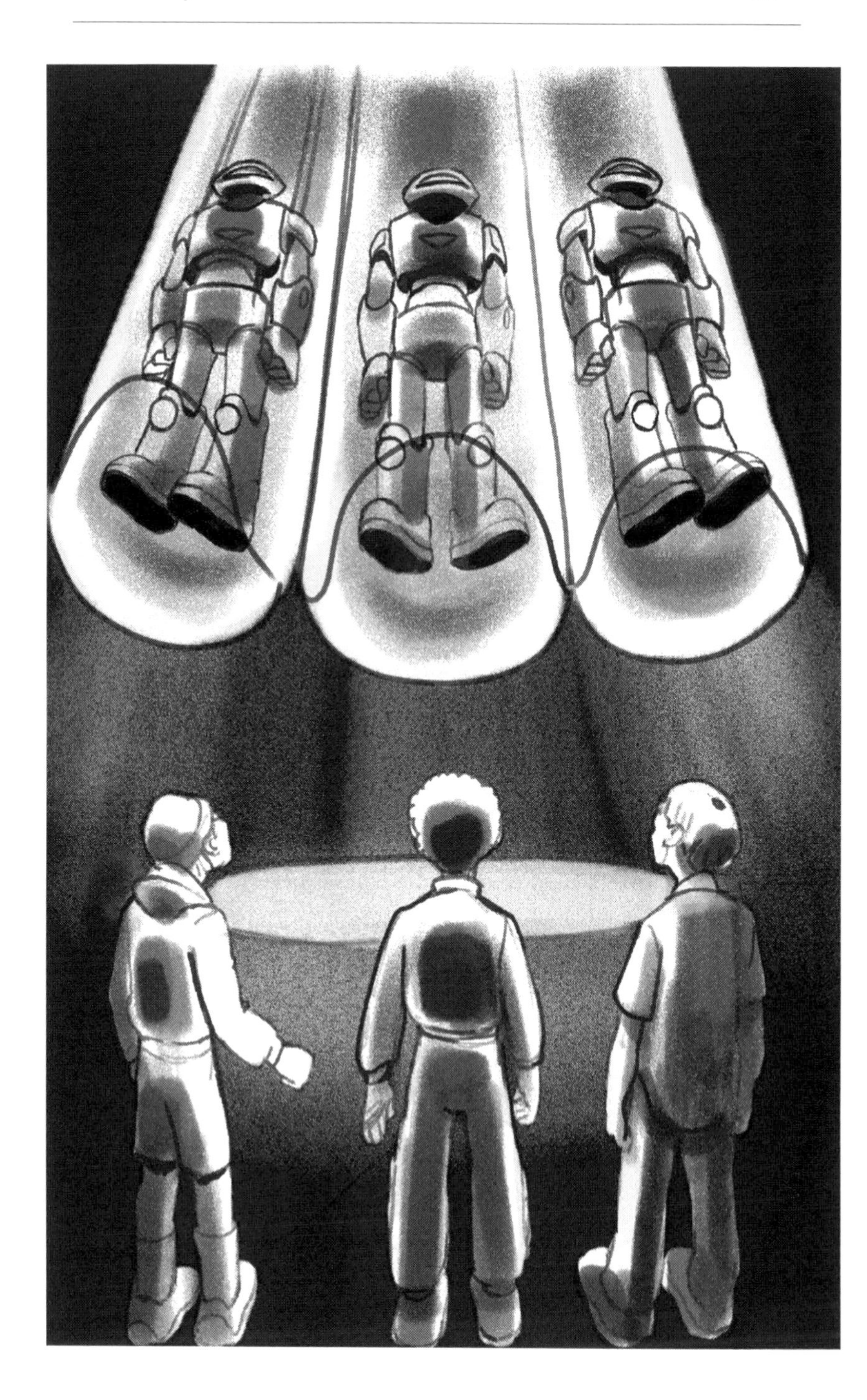

CHAPTER 10

Eliminate the intruders

Instinctively, they all jumped into a mech, just before the door was blasted open. Inside it was like a blue room. Garret was wearing some strange suit with all sorts of buttons and wires on it. He moved his hand and looked through the panel to see that his mech had done the same. He created a sword and out of nowhere one appeared on the robot's hand. He swished it around realising how light it was. He was just getting used to the robot's movement when the guards decided to attack.

They charged at them with laser swords drawn. He jumped to the side, sending a flurry of light waves into their eyes. They fell back blinded, and Garret took the opportunity to jump forward, punching one of the guards so hard that his titanium armour snapped and he flew out of the room.

The second guard had recovered his sight and sliced at the mech. Garret blocked the attack and elbowed him in the face. He then kicked the guard straight up into the air and finished him off with a roundhouse kick. The final guard was typing something on a small device. Garret shot a small beam frying it and the guard jumped back. He was just about to finish him when a danger signal on his mech appeared. ! HIGH POWER LEVEL ENEMY APPROACHING! That wasn't good. He stepped back and looked around. Where was it? He couldn't see anything; could it be an error in the system? Suddenly the floor started to rumble, his sensors telling him that something was coming from underground. Their mechs deactivated and he was shot out from the cockpit. Darvyn and Narvari, who had been watching the fight, put up a shield just before the impact. The ground exploded, rubble flying everywhere, and a man stepped out from the ground.

CHAPTER II

The battle is lost

He had sleek jet-black hair, flowing golden robes and a sly smile. They watched him warily.

"Are you Aeron Jnr?" Narvari asked.

"How could you tell?" Aeron Jnr chuckled. "Am I really that famous?"

"No, we are just here to stop you. We won't let you continue to kidnap the chosen ones!" Garret shouted.

"Well, well. See if you can then." Aeron Jnr smiled.

Garret lunged for him, sword slashing, but he wasn't there. He turned around to see Aeron Jnr behind him. Aeron gave him a solid punch and vanished again. Suddenly, he was in the air and hit Garret so hard that he heard a rib snap. Garrent wheezed and got up slowly, he started firing energy blasts instead, but Aeron Jnr dodged them just as easily. He created a flail and swung at him. Aeron caught it with two fingers, yanked it out Garret's hand and slammed the handle on his head. Garret fell straight to the floor, unconscious.

Darvyn gasped. "How is this possible? How are you so strong?"

"I guess you could say that I'm in a different league of power to you." Aeron jr stated.

"Well that doesn't matter, we will still defeat you." Darvyn shouted.

"Do your worst!" Aeron snarled.

Darvyn swung his fist with a charged gauntlet on it, at him. Aeron dodged the attack and tried to hit Darvyn, but he blocked it with a small electric shield. The lightning jolted through Aeron's body blasting him backwards with a big ZAP!

"Ha, got you!" Darvyn jeered.

"How...dare...you!" Aeron growled.

"Did that hurt, do you want me to call

your mummy!" Darvyn laughed. "It looks like I found your weakness. Once Garret wakes up, the only thing he will be hitting you with is electricity!"

"Then I guess I'll just stop him from waking up then," Aeron said.

Before they knew it, Aeron Jnr was next to Garret about to bring down a ginormous sword to impale him. Darvyn charged forward, but he realised that he was too far away. He looked around to Narvari for help, but he wasn't there.

CHAPTER 12

Teamwork makes the dream work

Maybe he had run away ... or maybe he was still with them. Darvyn turned on his x-ray vision.

There he was. Narvari crept behind Aeron jr. making sure that he wasn't heard. He wouldn't be able to heal Garret and get him to safety without being spotted, he needed Darv yn's help. How could he forget, he had telepathic power.

Darvyn! DARVYN!

Yes, I can hear you.

I need you to distract Aeron for me, so that I can heal Garret safely.

Alright. I have a plan

He created a small grenade and threw it to the side. It went off sending rubble and debris into the air. Aeron Jnr paused his attack and looked towards the explosion. He fired a few energy blasts where the grenade was and turned to face Garret. But Garret wasn't there. Aeron Jnr felt a whoosh of air and he was blasted forward. Garret hit him with his staff and sent a turret of electric blasts at him. The shots were hit away and Aeron Jnr charged at him. Aeron Jnr created a staff identical to Garret's one and they clashed. He swung and Garret deflected the attack. Garret infused the staff with electricity and fought more aggressively. He swung at Aeron Jnr's head and he blocked it, throwing a counter punch but Garret caught his hand, twisted him around, and slammed him to the ground. He followed through with a heavy attack. His electric staff hit him far back into a wall.

"Nice one Garret, you've got this!" Narvari shouted.

"Now to finish it in style!" Garret said.

He focused a ball of energy into the palms of his hands.

"KA-ME-HA-ME-HAAAAAAAAAAA!"

He fired the shot at Aeron. "Don't you go thinking that I am done. I still have one more move!" He bellowed.

"HA!"

Aeron Jnr fired his own blast, colliding with Garret's. They were even at first but Aeron Jnr was stronger. He pushed Garret's attack further back - Garret, what are you doing!

What do you mean Darvyn?

His weakness is electric

Oh yeah, how could I forget. But I can't, I can't muster enough energy to infuse this attack with electricity.

Damn, what can we do?

Well guess this is the part where I come in.

Narvari

Narvari

I can increase your power but I'm going to need Darvyn to support me okay.

Alright, let's do this

Narvari fired a continuous beam of magic into Garret, with Darvyn supporting him. The power difference was instantly noticeable. The blue energy beam had been mixed with purple and it was now growing bigger and bigger. Aeron Jnr's attack was weakening, and the despair was clear on his face. Garret finished off with a final blast destroying Aeon Jnr's attack and evaporating him on the spot. He was gone now and no more Chosen Ones would be taken ever again.

CHAPTER 13

The end to a new beginning

They called TDL over and the emergency team began to rescue the captured Chosen Ones.

"Wow, boys, I didn't think you would be able to do it!" TDL smiled.

"What, you thought we would fail. Then why did you send us?" Darvyn gasped.

"Well, we were watching you." He tapped a crystal. "In the end I think we all had a feeling that you would pull through. So, for your compensation -

"Oooh, how much is it? 10, 100, 1000!" Narvari gasped.

"It will be 1,000,000 metlet (alien currency)." TDL said.

"1 million metlet, we will be set for life!" They cheered.

But little did they know, it was the end to a new beginning.....

Printed in Great Britain
by Amazon

11345817R00039